A MAN AMONG THE MEN

PART 1 THE GOOD SALESMAN

ANNAMALAI SHANMUGANATHAN

Made with ❤ on the Notion Press Platform
www.notionpress.com

To the Divine, whose energy ignited the words on these
pages.

Contents

***

**

*

The Parallel Story

Contents

Foreword

Finally a debut attempt in English

&

It is A Fictional Story.
If you Feel yourself in this story, It is completely
Co-Incidence & Thank to my Imaginary Skills.

" I Am completely against drinking and It is my
personal opinion not influential to other"
For the one who believes the above sentence or
thinks like me -
Sorry I had written or created some instances of
drinking unavoidably to create the scene. Forgive Me!
Those who does not believe te above sentence -
"Drinking is Injurious To Health"

Acknowledgements

From the Heart:

Thank you **Ramesh Leela Shankar** -

My friend, well-wisher, and esteemed writer,

I cannot express my gratitude enough. If our paths had not crossed, I doubt I would have ever written a story in English.

Your English books have been a profound inspiration, igniting a passion for the language within me.

To the Brain:

Thanks to evolving technologies, I vividly recall writing my first novel in 2003 entirely by hand using a pencil and a school notebook. Unfortunately, due to limited exposure and financial constraints, I couldn't bring it to fruition.

After fire and the wheel, the internet is undoubtedly one of the most significant inventions in human history. While it won't physically increase the speed of Earth, it has revolutionized the way we live, communicate, and access information.

I am grateful for **online publishing platforms, Google,** and advanced language models like **Gemini,** which have made it possible for authors like me to share our work with a global audience.

To the Human Being:

Thank You **Ojas.** You are the Ignition point for this. This is (for) (because of) U.

Thank You **Shivshankar.** You helped me to ensure the flow & narration of story.

&

Thank You **Alamelu.**

Preface

When you hear the name "salesman," what comes to mind? A person who sells some product. It's very simple from our point of view. But a salesman needs to think from multiple angles to sell his product and get paid for his job.

When a salesman approaches you, it's your decision to buy or not from him. If you buy, you convert your money into a product; if you don't buy, you keep your money. Technically, there's no gain or loss for you.

But for a salesman, selling a product adds to his salary. If he doesn't sell, he needs one more customer. Most of the time, his salary is calculated based on the number of products he sells. His life is always tied to a rope called numbers: number of customers discovered, number of sales talks, number of products sold, and number of revenues generated. A thin rope of numbers is tied to his life kite. As the rope lengthens, he flies higher.

Every kite needs an initial thrust to fly up. That's the struggling period for all salesmen. Once he starts flying, he sees the entire world depends on the height he reaches. In other words, he has an eagle's eye. To get a view from his eagle's eye, he needs to be deaf, dumb, and blind at times. Many salesmen fail in their struggle, but many survive the battle.

This is not a sales story. I have obtained the title of sales man to this story and I dedicated this to all the salesmen who inspired me in my life.

- Annamalai Shanmuganathan

A Partial SWE (Salesman / Writer / Engineer)

Prologue

"You have to grow from the inside out. None can teach you, none can Make you spiritual. There is no other teacher but your own soul."

"In a conflict between the heart and the brain follow your heart"
- Swami Vivekananda

CHAPTER ONE

CHOTA CHIRAPUNJI

The Designer

AK - His name is Arunkumar, and friends call him AK as short for Arunkumar.

He's a 5-foot typical Indian man with a skin tone between black and brown. We can say a color of cappuccino.

He is short but he is having an extra-large brain. He always asks about and analyses everything he sees.

Sometimes this becomes irritating to his friends too, but he never minds. He keeps asking questions.

He believes that without a question, an answer never comes. Answers are derived only from questions.

He lives in Mumbai, the commercial capital and sleepless city of the nation.

He was born and brought up in Madurai, the cultural capital and sleepless city of the state Tamil Nadu.

Fifteen years ago, he was moved from a cultural capital to a commercial capital. Almost one and a half decades have passed for him in this commercial city.

He is a mature man, yet innocence and curiosity are ever-present in his endeavours. He believes that innocence and curiosity are making him more mature day by day.

According to AK, if we equate both words, "capital" becomes a common term, while "cultural" and "commercial" have distinct meanings. Nevertheless, for human survival, we need a balance between both cultural and commercial aspects.

Not only are there cultural differences, but there is also a difference in climate between these two cities.

Madurai gets a maximum average rainfall of 90 cm, whereas Mumbai gets 250 cm.

The highest and average rainfall in the nation is in Chirapunji, which is around 1400 cm. Comparing Madurai to Mumbai, he always calls Mumbai "Chotta Chirapunji" in terms of rain.

On one fine rainy day in Mumbai, he enjoyed the scenery of Powai Lake through his office window as it consumed rainwater and slowly expanded its circumference.

If you asked him, he could tell you the day-by-day volume of Powai Lake.

He's a MAD DESIGNER.

Between the vibrating sounds of raindrops hitting the earth, he heard the sound of vibration from his mobile.

His company's Travel admin was on the line. He picked the call.

"Yes. Arjun"

"AK, your Schengen visa has arrived! Let's plan your travel for the conference in Germany. can you please share some details to me. so that i can book the ticket"

A week ago, he applied for a Schengen visa to attend a conference in Nuremberg, Germany. He has never traveled to any country before, and this will be his first international trip.

"Sure Arjun. What are the details you need?"

"What's the date of your conference?"

"It's between 11-13th Monday to Wednesday of next month"

"So, you need to reach Germany on Sunday, it is 10th, and can start your return journey on 14th its Thursday. We'll book your tickets from Mumbai on Saturday evening, the 9th, and your return ticket from Nuremberg on the 14th. We'll plan the accommodations accordingly."

"Yes that will be fine"

"Okay, I'll look for options and send you the tickets. Please send me the details on Messenger or email. Also, please raise a ticket so that I can process it"

"Sure, Arjun. I've opened a ticket and you should receive a notification soon"

"Ok then. Bye AK"

"Bye Arjun"

Smaller hand in the AK's watch made its 15 steps and bigger hand completed it three and a half rounds.

The rain had stopped, and Powai Lake was enjoying the view of the naked blue sky.

AK was completely absorbed in his new circuit design calculations, oblivious to the scenery. Perhaps he didn't want to disturb the enjoyment of Powai Lake.

He received a notification pop-up.

An email with several attachments had arrived.

He opened the email and downloaded the attachments, which turned out to be his travel ticket and hotel accommodation. As he reviewed the documents, his eyebrows raised.

After carefully examining them, he called Arjun.

Hey Arjun, I saw your email. The return ticket is booked for Friday instead of Thursday."

"Yes, Thursday's flight was more expensive, so we booked it for Friday."

"Okay, but that means I'll have to stay an extra day, which will increase the cost, right?"

"We've calculated it, and it's actually cheaper this way. Plus, you'll get an extra day for sightseeing. Why are you worrying about all this? Just enjoy your trip, man."

AK smiled and replied, "That's fine. But you sent me someone else's hotel booking. I saw the name of OK on the booking slip."

"That's right. You're traveling with OK. He is also attending the conference."

"Oh my god! I have to travel with that Moto-G? Does he know about this?"

"No, AK. I need to inform him."

"Inform OK first."

AK's heart sank as he thought, "Everything will be okay from now on." A bitter irony in those words.

AK was feeling like a miniature version of Chirapunji, his mind churning like Powai Lake, unfortunately devoid of any clear sky.

AK's heart begins to feel heavy with the impending travel.

CHAPTER TWO

MOTO-JI

<u>The Sales man</u>

OK - Short form of "Ohm Krishna".

His father spelled his name as "Ohm" instead of "OM" because he wanted him to become an electrical engineer.

And indeed, he graduated as an electrical engineer, but he ultimately established himself as a successful salesman rather than an engineer.

He is a large, fair-skinned 5XL man with black hair. If his hair were a cappuccino colour, he might resemble a European.

As large as he is, he's also kind-hearted and skilled in sales.

Everyone calls him a good salesman, and he is one. He can sell anything.

His convincing skills are exceptional.

He prefers to listen more than talk.

He asks less questions.

He was born and brought up in Mumbai, enduring its natural and man-made calamities.

A mature and serious individual.

There is an innocence inside him, but it rarely surfaces

Tracing his growth. He started up his life in a short and sweet Mumbai Wala home and now he is experiencing a 2BHK life in Mumbai.

He has travelled extensively around the globe. He renewed his passport thrice.

He is the miles collector of his company.

There were two slots available for the Germany conference. Ak got the Visa and but the second person's visa was rejected. As a result, management decided to send OK instead, as he held a multiple-entry Schengen visa.

OK and AK often engage in discussions where they hold differing opinions.

OK sticks to a sales perspective, while AK focuses on design.

Their arguments were typically inconclusive.

Coming back to the situation - Powai Lake is looking the clear blue sky and OK's feeling vibration in his table.

Arjun's name was displaying his mobile phone. He attended the call in his Bluetooth neckband

"Yes Arji . Tell me"

Arjun was explaining the situation on the other side of the phone and a look of uneasiness appeared on OK's face.

"What? With that idiot? Why are you booking my tickets with him? You've even booked my stay with him!"

"The budget is exceeding limits, OK. What else can I do?"

"He'll ask infinite questions. You know what infinity means, right? I don't have any answers."

"OK, I know you, man. It's his first time traveling. I don't want to take risks. Better be with him."

"What can I do now? I'll go. Do I have any other options?"

"Relax Ok"

"It is decided. How can i able to make changes. I will go and i have to go. You send the tickets to me. i will talk to him and co-ordinate with him"

"Thanks Ok. Take care of him"

"Don't worry you will get your designer back"

Rain started Again and Powai Lake started increasing its Circumference.

OK decided to travel with him as there were no other options. The two are polar opposites in every way.

Like poles always repel each other, but these opposite poles are about to embark on a journey together.

Let's see how the law of attraction will play out.

Result could be Either AK vs OK or AK & OK.

TERMINA-L-TOR

<u>Airport:</u>

The Name is Chhatrapati Sivaji Maharaj International Airport

In short it is called as Terminal 2 and it is situated 3 km southeast of Powai Lake.

It was awarded the title of Best International Airport in 2012 and 2020.

As the second busiest airport in the nation, it processes an average of 980 flights per day, meaning a flight takes off or lands every 88 seconds.

The airport is served by 63 international airlines and offers 108 aircraft parking stands, 60 boarding bridges, 192 check-in counters, and 5000 car parking spaces.

It is the fifth largest airport in the country by area, although it handles an impressive 4 crore people annually, which is nearly 3% of India's population.

An average of 1.1 lakh people pass through the airport daily, with approximately 4,500 people using the airport every hour.

And AK is one of the 4,500 people who passed through this airport during the 18th hour of the ninth day of that month.

AK didn't know what to do in the crowd, so he called OK.

"OK, I have reached the airport."

"Which terminal are you at? 1 or 2?"

AK was a bit confused and looked around until he found a board indicating T2.

"I'm in T2. The ticket says T2 too. Any change in the flight?" AK became more confused.

"No, no. This isn't a railway platform where numbers got change in the last moment. I was just checking if you arrived correctly."

AK relaxed. "Okay, okay. Where are you now? What time will you reach?"

"My home is nearby. I'll start in a few minutes. Show your passport and ticket at the security counter and go inside. Wait in the hall after the gate. I'll pick you up."

"Okay. Which gate number should I go to? There are four gates here."

"You can go to any. You just need proper ID and a ticket."

"ID and ticket? Can I show my Aadhaar card?"

"Yes, you can."

"Then why do I need to show my passport?" OK got tense with his question.

"Your passport is also an ID, that's why."

"If i Show Aadhaar then i don't need to show passport right?"

OK's tension increased further with his question "Don't ask too many questions. Go inside and watch a movie on your phone. I'll come."

"I don't have any movies on my phone, man." AK casually responded

OK's irritation peaked as he shouted, "Then listen to some songs. Don't tell me you don't have any songs!" and immediately hung up. He started thinking about how he was going to survive with AK for the next week.

AK stood in the queue, showed his Aadhaar card and ticket, and went inside.

There were ten huge pillars inside the airport labelled A to J. Several airline counters were located near these pillars, with each pillar assigned to specific airlines.

AK, who thought metro stations were more beautiful than railway stations, was impressed by the airport. He started wandering from pillar A to J, observing the people.

AK usually travelled by train whenever he went to his hometown, Madurai.

Crossing three states with three different languages, he encountered diverse people and cultures during his train journeys.

He passed through three major railway stations before reaching home. However, the airport was a stark contrast.

Unlike railway stations where passengers often rely on porters to handle luggage due to platform heights, everyone at the airport managed their own bags using trolleys.

The airport's design eliminated the need to climb stairs or escalators.

There were no unpleasant odours, and even the restrooms were scented.

Moreover, the airport was remarkably quiet with huge crowd.

Just minutes earlier, he had been struggling with his bag on the crowded Ghatkopar urban railway station, only to transfer to the equally noisy metro.

The sudden quiet of the airport was like putting on noise-cancelling headphones in the ear.

AK enjoyed watching the people passing by. After about an hour, he called OK.

""OK, have you arrived?"

"No. I am leaving now, just listen some more songs" OK replied, hanging up the call.

AK continued watching the people. Another hour passed before he called OK again. His voice tinged with impatience "OK. How long it will take"

"I'm on the way. There's a bit of traffic. Listen to some more songs" OK responded casually and ending the call.

AK was waiting for a long time, and he was starting to get really mad.

Every fifteen minutes, AK started calling OK.

OK didn't pick up the call.

As a payback for AK's irritating questions, OK ignored him.

AK's irritation reached its peak.

OK finally picked up the call after an hour.

"Where are you, OK? I've been calling you crazy!"

"Why are you calling so crazy? You can call normally."

"Stop fooling around. Where are you? We're going to be late!"

"We are not late, Turn back"

AK turned around in surprise to find OK standing nearby.

"Why did it take you so long, OK?"

"Why did you come so early, AK?"

"How can you say I'm early?"

"What time is our flight?"

"It's at 11:00 PM."

"For an 11:00 PM flight, why did you get here at 6:00 PM?"

"My uncle said we need to be there three hours early for international travel."

"Correct and still 11 minus 3 is 8. Why did you come two hours early? Is it your design tolerance?"

"No, I added a little cushion."

"So I was squeezing your cushion."

AK was speechless, and OK had finally gotten his revenge.

OK continued with smile, "Come on, let's go. We don't have any more cushion, and I don't want to squeeze you any further, my friend." AK smiled after hearing the words from Ok and followed him in the Busiest Airport.

It was raining outside and Powai Lake is increasing its circumference.

CHAPTER FOUR

BOARDING TIME

OK was heading to the Air Bhaarath counter with his luggage bag, followed by AK. Luckily, the counter was not crowded. OK gave his passport and ticket to the in-charge.

She checked the ticket, passport, and visa details, then turned to OK with a smile.

"Sir, your full name, please?"

"Ohm Krishna."

"You are traveling to?"

"Munich."

"Ok, sir. Do you have any cabin luggage with you?"

"Yes."

"Sir, please keep the luggage here."

OK lifted his bag and placed it on the conveyor. It weighed 12 kg. An idea struck OK, and he turned to AK. "It's only 12 kg, and we still have 13 more kg to spare. Give me your bag too. We can put them together and save time."

OK thought this would reduce the process time for AK if he didn't have any separate luggage.

AK agreed and put his bag on the conveyor. Now the weight was 20 kg. OK was surprised. "You don't have much weight in it, it seems," he said. AK nodded.

The in-charge girl continued, "Sir, make sure there is no power bank, batteries, flammable liquid items, or any toxic content in the bag."

OK thought for a second, then turned to AK. "Did you put your power bank in the luggage bag?"

"If I put the power bank inside, how could I charge my phone?"

"Just answer yes or no. Why are you rambling?"

"No... Happy?"

OK shook his head and said. "Very happy,"

OK turned back to the in-charge and said, "No."

She printed out stickers, placed them on the bag, and handed the boarding pass to OK.

"Sir, your flight is at gate 58. Your boarding time is 10:10 you have 40 minutes from now. You can proceed to the security check-in and then immigration."

She smiled and pressed a button, starting the luggage on its way.

OK moved aside and told AK to give his ticket to the girl.

AK gave his ticket and Aadhaar card to the girl.

She looked at the ticket and asked, "Sir, your passport, please."

AK was surprised and turned back to ok and said "You said we had to show ID card and ticket. Why are they asking for a passport?"

OK got irritated. "Why are you asking questions? Just give them what they ask for."

"At security they let me in with my Aadhaar card. Why do I need a passport now?"

"AK, are you a kid? This is to verify your visa. Give them the passport. We don't have time."

"OK, I don't have my passport with me."OK was stunned by what he heard"

"What? You don't have passport with you? Where is it then?"

"It's in my luggage bag. It went in."

OK felt a mountain of pressure on his mind "Why did you put it in your luggage bag?"

"You said we had to show Aadhaar and ticket. I thought it wasn't needed, so I put it inside."

Every answers of AK added a mountain to Ok's Pressure "Why didn't you tell me when she asked for it?"

"You asked about the power bank, not the passport." again a mountain to OK

OK's anger was rising more than the height of Everest. He didn't know what to do.

He paused, closed his eyes, and took a few deep breaths. Everest reduced its height to Western Ghats.

Then he opened his eyes and asked the girl politely,

"Ma'am, can you please bring the luggage back? There's a problem. He put his passport inside. We need to call back forget his passport. We have no other option. Can you please help us?"

That girl was about to laugh. But she controlled her laughter and she calmly replied, "Give me a minute to check."

She was calling his assistant and informed him to check the baggage status. She took her walkie talkie and was informing something in it.

OK was seeing AK and with his sight of eyes, he could have killed him. If someone wants to witness a volcano erupting in a human eye, OK's eyes are the same.

After a minute, the girl received a call on her landline. After disconnecting the call, she said,

"Sir, your luggage didn't go inside. We're holding it, but I need to cancel the boarding pass and redo the process. You might have to give a formal letter for this. Is that okay?"

"I don't have a choice, madam, because I already took him with me without any choice, please give me a pen and paper"

OK gave a letter to the airline, and they brought back the luggage, removed the tags, and finally, AK took his passport from the bag.

The process took 30 minutes, and finally, both of them got their boarding passes.

OK was trying to take a shortcut to reduce the time by 3 minutes but it turned into a 30-minute delay.

OK realised this act of karma. OK didn't say anything and walked towards the security counter.

AK was following him. AK felt really bad about this.

He walked forward, held OK's hand, and stopped him.

OK turned back.

AK said politely, "I'm sorry, OK. I should have been more cautious. Because of me, you had to give an apology letter. I'll make sure this doesn't happen again."

The words came from his heart, and his eyes were filled with apologies.

More than words, eyes and mind can communicate faster. A heartfelt sorry can dissolve many angers. With his apology, OK's anger departed from his mind.

He smiled at AK and said very politely, "it's okay. Come, let's go. We need to explore a lot."

Both walked towards the security gate.

This time, OK was cautious and explained everything clearly to AK.

Both of them passed security and moved to the immigration gate.

Again, OK explained everything to AK.

He told AK to go first because he wanted to make sure that he would pass the gate without any problem. There was a crowd in all the lines.

OK informed AK to follow him.

He moved to the physically challenged person counter as it was free, and only one person was in the examining officer's cabin.

AK asked OK, "Ohm, we are in the physically challenged person counter."

"Yeah, I know. We can stand here also, but the priority will be for the physically challenged person. If nobody is there, we are allowed to go," OK replied.

As he said this, the officer called AK as nobody was behind them. OK was nervous watching AK.

The officer asked AK, "Your name, please."

"Arun Kumar," AK replied.

"Where are you traveling to?"

"Germany."

"Which place in Germany?"

"Nuremberg."

"Purpose of your visit?"

"Conference."

The officer put the immigration seal in the passport and gave the passport and boarding pass back to him. AK was happy. More than him, OK was very happy. But one thing he forgot was that they had crossed the boarding t-i---m-----e.

It is 10:30 now.

CHAPTER FIVE

RABBIT &
RHINOCEROS

OK realized they had crossed the boarding time and there was no chance of getting on the plane.

Still, OK informed AK, "You go faster towards gate 58, go straight and follow the signboard. Airline staff will be there. Tell them we need to board the plane. Go faster, I'm following you."

OK couldn't walk with his large size, so he urged AK to run.

AK was running like a rabbit, and OK was following him like a rhinoceros through the airport.

AK reached the gate three minutes later and saw it was closed. Air Bhaarath Lady was standing there. She was talking to someone. AK wait for minute till she turns into his side. He showed his boarding pass.

She had a look into that boarding pass and said "Sir, you need to wait until 1:00 PM," she said.

Ak was confused and turned around just as Ok arrived.

"OK, they're saying we have to wait three hours," Ak explained, sounding bewildered.

Ok was surprised. "Are they planning to put us on the next flight? No chance. The next flight is tomorrow. Wait, let me ask her."

OK walked up to the staff and asked, "What happened, madam? Any chance of boarding now?"

"No, sir. The flight is delayed for three hours," she replied.

Ok was even more surprised "What? I didn't get any message or call. Even your display is showing the real time."

"Yes, sir. There was a technical error. That's why there were no SMS notifications and the display wasn't updated. We're standing here to inform passengers. Sorry for the inconvenience. We'll arrange drinks and food soon. Please wait, sir," she explained.

Ok took a deep breath and said loudly, "Thank you, madam. Thank you so much."

He turned to AK. "Hey, debut traveller, I thought you were bowled out on your first ball. Luckily, it's a no-ball." and started smiling.

AK was confused. "Oh, sir, I'm still panicking. Don't confuse me further. Are we boarding the plane or not? Please answer directly."

"Hey friend, the flight is delayed. We're going to board after 1:00 PM. Come on, let's make a plan." Ok cleared his confusion.

"What plan?" AK didn't understand

"Nothing, just come with me. We'll go shopping." Said OK and he started walking on the direction they came.

As the rhinoceros started moving, and the rabbit followed.

OK took him to the duty-free counter. A salesgirl in the duty-free shop came to him and said, "Yes sir, how can I help you?"

"Any offers today?" Ok asked.

"Yes sir, we have 1+1 offers on Blue Label. With GPay, you'll get an additional 10% off."

"Exceeding the budget, madam. Any other offers less than 10K?"

"Less than 10K... yes sir, we have Chivas. Same 1+1 and 10% extra on GPay."

"What is the price of it?"

"Chivas Regal 15, 1+1. Today the price is 7999."

OK didn't listen to the girl and was watching the announcement display for the flight timing. It was still showing the old time. Suddenly he realized that the girl was saying the price and asked her politely, "Sorry madam, can you repeat it once? I didn't notice. Sorry."

The girl smiled and replied, "No problem, sir. Chivas Regal 15, 1+1, it's 7999, and you will get a 10% discount through GPay, so it will be 7199."

"It's a good deal. Please book the order, I will pay in advance and I need it while returning."

"OK, sir, no problem. Your passport and boarding pass, please, and return ticket, please."

OK gave her the boarding pass, passport, and return ticket. She checked the ticket and said, "So your return is on the 15th, right?"

"Yes."

She entered all the details in her iPad and said, "Order booked. Please scan the QR code and make the payment, sir."

"I will pay by card."

"It will be 800 rupees extra by card."

"No problem, madam. I'm buying it for my friend, so I will collect it from him. Why are you reducing 800 rupees in your turnover?" Ok replied smartly and smiled.

The girl smiled immediately and said, "No issues, sir, as you wish."

She went inside and brought the swiping machine. AK swiped and entered the PIN. He got a message receipt from duty-free.

The girl continued, "Sir, you may have received a message, and you need to show this message, passport, and return boarding pass at the arrival duty-free counter and collect your item."

"No problem, madam. Thank you."

OK once again saw the display board and the flight time was updated now. It was 1:00 PM, and the boarding tie will be 12:15 time was now 11:45 PM. He is having another 30 minutes.

OK noticed one thing. AK was missing. He searched for him in the shop but couldn't find him anywhere.

He took his mobile phone and dialled his number. A Tamil song was playing as the caller tune. The caller tune finished. He didn't pick up the call. He called him thrice, but he didn't answer.

AK was not in his vicinity. He panicked again.

The rhinoceros had lost the rabbit now.

As a result of peak anger he don't want to go on search mode and He decided that he will board the flight without him and started walking.

The Rhinoceros started moving towards gate 58 without the Rabbit.

CHAPTER SIX

WILLKOMMEN IN DEUTSCHLAND

OK slowly walked and reached gate 58.

He was looking for a seat to sit and noticed that AK was sleeping in a chair in that area, snoring like a bike engine.

OK went near him and, gathering all his anger, gave him a push.

AK woke up suddenly and noticed OK.

"Hey, you came? How was the chat with that girl? All good?" he asked in a teasing manner.

OK got angry and started shouting on him "I am going to slap you. You came here and didn't inform me. I was searching for you, and your number is switched off."

AK shoed his innocence in his face and replied "No... I dropped you a message on WhatsApp. You're seriously talking to that girl, so I didn't want to disturb you. So I sent a WhatsApp message to you and came here," he was giving his phone to OK to see the message.

OK took his phone, had a look and showed back to AK, and said, "You sent a message on WhatsApp, but your phone was in flight mode. You didn't notice it."

"Sorry, yaar, I kept it in silent mode during security check. I forgot to release. I was feeling sleepy also. So I didn't realize." Again he replied with innocence

"Every time you say sorry. Sorry never corrects mistakes." OK feeling annoyed.

"I know. But I will correct mistakes. I never do repeated mistakes. Don't worry."

"Your first time mistakes are very hard to handle. Don't ever think of repeating them. And please don't make mistakes."

"Relax, OK. Come and sit."

OK sat near him. After 15 minutes, the boarding started.

Both boarded the plane.

As usual, OK booked an aisle seat for legroom, while AK got the middle seat.

The window seat was empty, and no one claimed it by the end of boarding.

OK told AK, "You can take the window seat. Nobody's going to come."

"What if someone comes at the next stop?" AK asked childishly.

OK didn't know whether to laugh or get angry. "I've already told you this isn't a train, it's a plane. The next stop is Munich. So sit there," he replied.

"So it's a non-stop flight?" again he asked childishly.

"Yes All flights are non-stop like Kalyan Fast local train. Can you please move and sit?" OK explained in his style,

AK agreed, moved to the window seat, and fastened his seatbelt. He watched over 25 YouTube short videos on how to wear a seatbelt and successfully passed the practical test.

The plane raced down the runway like Usain Bolt.

As it neared the end, it balanced lift and gravity on one side with thrust and drag on the other.

It lifted off the ground and began to soar through the air.

The plane flew over Mumbai, passing Powai Lake. As usual Powai Lake was looking into the blue sky with a plane passing on.

AK was so tired that he fell asleep immediately, snoring like a bike engine.

OK inserted noise-cancelling plugs into his ears and tried to sleep.

A few minutes later, AK's snoring escalated to the sound of an old diesel car engine.

Modern car engines are much quieter, so OK was slightly disturbed but managed to stay asleep.

Soon, the snoring resembled an old diesel generator.

This time, OK was fully awake and saw AK snoring loudly.

He gently pushed him. AK woke up, saw OK, and fell back asleep almost instantly.

Within minutes, his snoring was louder than the plane's engine. OK couldn't sleep for the rest of the night.

The plane soared above borders, and AK's snores echoed over those nations.

After six and half hours the plane landed in Munich. Everybody started moving out from the plane including OK & AK.

After six hours of sleep AK feels slightly tired and OK feels ------.

Both came to the immigration gate. OK was very careful and instructed AK how to answer the questions.

There were 10 cabins for the immigration and after the cabin there was an exit door. Once the visa is approved they will open the exit door and the person can go into the nation.

Both of them were standing in the queue. AK went to cabin no 9 and OK went to cabin no 10.

Officer was asking questions to AK.

"What is the purpose of your visit to Germany?"

"I am here to attend the conference."

"How long will you be staying in Germany?"

"Five days."

"When is your return ticket?"

"It's on the tenth, sir."

"Okay. Have a Nice trip"

The officer placed the immigration seal in his passport and opened the gate.

While coming out of the gate, AK got stunned by what he was seeing.

OK was taken by some officers to the enquiry room. He did not understand anything.

The police officer near the entry gate was urging AK to move out. He asked the officer, "Why are they taking him there?"

"Oh, that's the enquiry room. If the visa is denied, they will take the passenger to that room. Please move ahead," the officer replied.

AK didn't know what to do and stand there for some seconds. Officer shouted on him.

Without any options he moved out of the immigration hall.

AK's head was aching more. He was alone in the unknown nation. Unsure of what to do he was walking slowly without consciousness.

A board came into sight outside the immigration room with the sentence

"Willkommen in Deutschland," meaning **"Welcome to Germany"**

CHAPTER SEVEN

WILLKOMMEN IN MÜNCHEN

AK was standing still outside the immigration gate.

He did not know what to do next. He waited near the gate for more than fifteen minutes, expecting OK to come out at any cost. OK didn't come out.

He decided to move alone after waiting for a long time.

OK had explained him about the formalities to do after immigration. OK had told him to collect the baggage. He followed the signs moved towards the baggage collection centre.

He could see his baggage on the moving conveyor belt.

AK collected his baggage and sat down on a waiting chair kept near the baggage area.

His head was filled with a lot of thoughts. He was waiting for some more time as he believes Ok will come.

'Six hours ago, OK had decided to travel alone, leaving him behind. It felt like a bad turn of events. Karma is a boomerang.'

Thirty minutes gone. OK didn't come. No matter what happened, show has to run. AK gathered his courage and decided to continue alone.

He was in Munich now and needed to go to Nuremberg.

He checked his tickets and found one for the Munich to Nuremberg. He was searching for the entry to next flight. He started checking the signboards, after finding the domestic transfer place, he went there and showed the ticket to an officer.

The officer look at the ticket and said it was a bus ticket and he needed to leave through the exit gate.

AK was confused. He thought he'd need to take another flight. But he realized that this is a bus ticket he had to take a bus. But still he wondering why they are giving boarded passes for busses also?

He started leaving the airport through Exit gate. As he is leaving the airport, he looked around for OK but couldn't find him.

He came out of the Airport. A Sign board welcoming him with its word **Willkommen in München** Meaning **Welcome to Munich.**

The weather was freezing. Outside, temperature is 2 Degree Celsius and it was very cold.

In general we need three layer of winter protection to protect our self from the cold.

Shivering in the cold, he pulled on his winter jacket.

He was hungry. He was searching for restaurant and found a Starbucks in the departure area, He went there and got confused with the menu. Simply he ordered a cappuccino and a burger.

The total came to 29 euros, which was roughly 300 rupees.

He compare it to the 28 rupees he'd spend on tea and a vada-pav in Mumbai. It was ten times the price.

He gave three 10-euro notes, received a one-euro coin as change, and found a seat directly opposite the exit gate.

Sitting there, he watched the exit, hoping to see OK, but there was no sign of him.

Lost in thought, he finished his coffee and burger.

Suddenly, he realized he hadn't called OK.

He quickly grabbed his phone and dialled his number, but found that OK's phone was switched off.

All the gates are closed for OK and AK.

AK came out of the coffee shop and asked a policeman for directions to the bus stop.

The officer looked at his boarding pass and pointed him towards a pathway.

AK thanked him and followed the path.

He passed by electronics stores, a mini-market, brand-name clothing shops, and finally a pizza place.

After that was an open area where several buses were parked.

He checked the buses for signs but couldn't find any.

Approaching the first bus driver, he showed the boarding pass.

The driver checked it and said it was for the third bus.

That third bus was about to leave.

He ran quickly and showed his boarding pass to the driver.

The driver was shouting something in German.

He didn't understand the language, but realized the driver was angry with him for being late.

Germans are very punctual.

The bus was scheduled to leave at 8:00 AM and it was now 8:03 AM.

The driver opened the luggage compartment and he put his bag inside before getting on the bus. It was full, except for two seats.

AK took one of them. AK knew the empty seat was for OK, who couldn't enter Germany.

The bus left the bus bay and started moving towards the exit.

He felt bad for OK, who hadn't arrived.

The bus came to a sudden stop as somebody stepped in front of it.

The driver started yelling in German to that person.

AK realized something was wrong at the bus station.

He felt confused and upset.

AK wondered how many problems he'd have to deal with in Germany.

His colleague got denied entry, he got confused with Airline and Bus Boarding pass, and after difficulty he found the bus and got scolded for his late entry.

His first international trip was turning out to be a nightmare.

With all his confusions he was looking into the driver seat.

After a few conversations he pressed a button in the bus and the door got opened.

He could not realise the scenery.

'OK alias Ohm Krishna' was walking towards him on the bus, looking like Lord 'Shri Krishna' and said

Willkommen in München.

CHAPTER EIGHT

WILLKOMMEN IN NÜRNBERG

AK was shocked and didn't realize that OK was sitting next to him.

Tears started to flow from AK's eyes.

OK calmed him down, saying, "Don't be like a kid."

"I'm not a kid," AK replied. "I can't control my feelings. I'm really happy you came back." Ak cleared his tears from the eyes.

"It's okay, man. These things happen on international trips. I'll explain what happened. Relax first,"

The bus left the airport and entered the highway.

A digital display inside the bus showed the time and temperature. It was 8:08 AM and 3 degrees Celsius.

A 22-inch television screen displayed a map of the route from Munich to Nuremberg.

AK asked, "What happened?"

OK began to explain what had happened at the immigration counter.

✳ ✳ ✳

Munich – Immigration

OK handed his passport to the examining officer and glanced towards counter 9 where AK was answering questions.

The officer at counter 10 turned to OK. And asked "Your name, please?"

"Ohm Krishna," OK replied.

"Purpose of your visit?"

"I'm here to attend a conference in Nuremberg," he answered.

The officer carefully examined the passport, flipping through its pages.

He then opened three older passports belonging to OK and studied them.

"What is your profession?"

"I am in sales."

"What is the purpose of your visit?"

"I am here to attending a conference"

"What is the conference you are going to attend here"

"It is a tech conference"

"Why does a salesperson need to attend a technical conference?" Officer asked him with a doubt.

"My company sent me to this conference to learn about technical things. That's why I am here." OK Replied

"I'm sorry, sir. I cannot accept your visa. You must return to your country" officer replied in a refusing manner.

OK interrupted the officer and said "Excuse me, This conference is very important to me. I need to go. Please allow me?."

"NO. I cannot permit you, if you need you can discuss with my seniors, if they permits you can, but I cannot permit you." Officer replied.

"Will you allow me to meet your senior? Please" Ok asked in a polite manner.

He called two officers to escort him inside.

They escorted him and that time AK was noticing this.

Ohm was waiting in the enquiry room. After five minutes the superior officer arrived.

"How can i help you?"

"Sir, my visa has been denied. Could you please explain the reason for this decision?"

"Give me your passport please"

Ohm handed his passport to the officer. The officer input the details into the computer, carefully read the report for a minute, and then said...

""We've reviewed your passport and noticed a recent visit to Russia. Given the current tensions between Russia and European nations, and your role as a salesperson attending a technical conference, we're unable to justify your entry at this time. Do you have any specific information or documentation that could clarify this situation and help us reconsider your application?""

"Yes sir. I have" Ohm replied confidently.

"Please go ahead"

"With your permission can i open my laptop?"

"Yes please"

Ohm took out his laptop and opened it. He found a specific email, showed it to the officer, and began to explain.

"Please read this email. My company sent me to this conference because I'm the salesperson responsible for selling this product in my country. I need to learn about the product to successfully market it. If I secure an order, it will lead to exports from Germany. Denying my entry would indirectly reduce revenue for both our countries."

The officer listened intently, read the email, and returned the laptop.

"This is acceptable, but your recent visit to Russia is a concern. Our policy is to avoid supporting individuals with ties to Russia. Therefore, I must uphold my decision."

Ohm smiled confidently, opened another email, and showed it to the officer.

"Sir, please read this email. It's a letter confirming the closure of our business with a Russian company. I visited Russia to finalize the closing documents. Furthermore, my company has terminated all business relationships with Russian companies, I am ensuring that I won't be travel to Russia."

The officer studied the email and documents intently.

"This business closure caused our company a revenue loss of 10 million euros, which is 10% of our annual income. We're actively seeking new business opportunities in European countries, and that's why I'm here."

"I understand your situation. I'll grant you entry into the country with a limited stay. Your return ticket is on the 14th, so I'll approve your visa until the 15th of this month. Is that acceptable?"

"More than enough sir"

Officer granted visa to Ohm.

Ohm rushed out like a rhinoceros and grabbed his phone to call AK. Unfortunately, his phone was dead. He pulled out a power bank from his bag and started charging the lifeless device.

He grabbed his luggage and left the airport. Feeling hungry, he bought coffee and a burger at Starbucks.. For the same 29 Euro bill he swiped his card.

He walked towards the pathway, coffee and burger in hand. From a distance, he saw AK getting on a bus.

He walk faster with his rhinoceros speed and stop the bus like a rhinoceros.

*** * ***

AK listened carefully without blinking. He said, "You were really confident. You told the officer that he was stopping business between two countries."

Ohm replied, "It's true. We represent our country. If our company gets a deal, it brings in revenue, which directly contributes to India's economy. All the success in international sales will make our nation's revenue stronger."

AK was very proud of Ohm. "Your father named you perfectly. You're very resistive. From now on, I'll call you Ohm instead of OK"

No problem," Ohm replied, laughing. "But don't forget to follow Ohm's law." AK joined in the laughter.

Their conversation ended as the bus arrived at Nuremberg Airport, where a welcoming sign read, **"Willkommen in Nürnberg"**

CHAPTER NINE

THE 9TH MAN

Both of them got down at Nuremberg airport.

It was a very calm airport, less crowded and about the size of a tier-two railway station in India.

AK asked Ohm, "If Nuremberg has an airport, then why did we come by bus?"

"The distance is very short, so there aren't frequent flights. That's why we travelled by bus," Ohm explained.

"Okay, what next? Do we need to take Ola or Uber from here?" Ak asked.

"Nope. Taxis are very costly. We'll take the metro," Ohm replied.

AK looked up and around, searching for the metro. "There's no metro here," he said.

Ohm understood. "Don't look up. In Mumbai, the metro is elevated, but here everything is underground. See that blue sign with a 'U'? Written with Flughafen. That's for the metro station. 'Flughafen' means airport in German." Ohm pointed to a blue signboard that read "Flughafen".

"Oh!" AK exclaimed, looking surprised. They both walked towards the board, with AK moving faster in excitement. Rhinoceros followed the rabbit.

AK reached the board and saw an escalator moving downwards. But the entrance was protected by an automatic gate.

Turning to Ohm, AK asked, "Where's the ticket counter? It seems we need to get the ticket outside."

"Not 'seems,' we need to," Ohm replied

"But where is the ticket counter?" AK asked again.

Ohm pointed his finger towards a 40 inch vertical display near the station.

AK looked surprised. "What are you saying? This is an airport metro, and there's no ticket counter? We need to get a ticket from this small machine?"

Ohm nodded.

AK approached the machine, which was completely in German. Confused, he looked at Ohm.

Ohm gently pushed AK and pointed to the bottom corner of the display. There was an 'EN' sign. He touched it, and the display changed to English.

He bought the tickets and tapped his card on the machine. Two hard paper tickets were printed. He gave one to AK and said, "Follow me."

Ohm moved towards the gate and told AK watch what i am doing.

Ohm moved towards the gate and told AK to watch. There was a box with a slot at the entrance. Ohm inserted the ticket, and the gate opened. After going through, the ticket was returned with the entry time printed on it. This is to track the time you have entered in the station.

AK followed what Ohm did.

Both entered the escalator. AK was in front of Ohm and stood on the left side.

Ohm tapped his shoulder and said, "Stand on the right side. People who are walking use the left."

AK moved to the right side of the escalator.

As the escalator moved, a man walked past AK on the left side and continued walking on the left without moving to the right. Similarly two more people did. AK was impressed by the people's discipline.

Both reached Line 2, where a train was waiting on the platform.

It was the starting station for this line.

They boarded the first compartment, and Ak was surprised.

There was no attendant or driver. It was completely automated.

"What is this? Is it an automated metro system?" Ak asked.

"Yes, this is GoA 4," Ohm replied.

"What is GoA 4? Is there another version of our Goa in Germany?" AK joked.

Ohm got irritated. "Stop with the stupid jokes. This is Grade of Automation 4 which needs no human intervention. , there is another grade called GoA3 which need less human control."

"What we have in India?"

"Our country has mostly GoA 3 metros, Delhi launched it in 2018, Mumbai in 2022"

"So we are also advancing"

"Not exactly. Munich has had it since 2008, so we're about 10 years behind them. Actually, it was first launched in Paris in 1998, putting us about 20 years behind the world, and our neighbour implemented in 2020 so we are two years ahead of our neighbours," Ohm said with a smile.

By the time during discussion the train departed and AK was standing in front of the compartment and he is getting a feel of driving the metro train.

In another 20 minutes they have reached the destiny railway station and they claimed the escalators and this time AK stand in the right side properly, people moving in the left side.

While coming out AK placed the ticket the slot. The gate opened and gave the ticket printed with the out time. This is to track the exit time of the station.

After coming out of the station, AK said to Ohm, "In one thing, I'm very happy, Ohm."

"What?" Ohm asked.

"We are two years ahead of our neighbours," AK replied.

After hearing this, Ohm responded with a slightly angry tone, "There are ten people running a race. You're one of them, and with the potential to be in the top three, you finished ninth and are happy about beating the tenth person. Is that right?"

"Ohm, you mean to say..." AK began.

Ohm interrupted, "Change your mind-set. Everything will change automatically, and we'll show the world what GoA 5 is."

This Time Rhinoceros walked like a Lion.

JEDEME DO PRAHY

Three days of the conference went well in Nuremberg. AK and Ohm enjoyed their time together.

At the end of the conference, they decided to have a party. AK asked Ohm about a good place to drink.

Ohm said, "There's a party place. We'll go in the evening."

Time was around 7 PM. Sunset happened at 5.00 PM itself after 5 it is completely dark.

Ohm took AK to a hotel called Part E, the fifth branch of a chain owned by an Indian.

The first hotel was called Part A, the second Part B, and so on.

The hotel was empty. In the corner, a 42-inch Samsung TV was mounted on the wall, playing the Indian song "Dilbar." from the Movie SatyaMeva Jayate.

Ohm found a place to sit and ordered beer, and AK did the same.

While ordering, Ohm asked the waiter for a card machine. He paid immediately.

AK asked, "Why?"

"My card always gives trouble after ordering," Ohm explained. "I don't know why. So, I pay upfront. You weren't there at the duty-free when I pre-booked drinks and paid in advance to avoid card problems."

AK laughed at Ohm's logic.

Ohm started explaining "AK stop laughing, each and every person has their own sentiments. You know one thing, my boss taken my earphones whenever he travels to other country or attending any new customers"

"Do you have a good earphone with you?" AK Asked

"He thinks it's lucky," Ohm replied

"Did he told that to you?" AK asked

"Yes. When he was taking his fifth peg" Ohm started laughing louder and continued "you will see a person who thinks like me"

The beer arrived, and they started drinking. After a few minutes, AK said, "I need to take a bio break. I'll be back soon." Ohm laughed, "Take a bio break, but don't break the bio!"

Ohm continued drinking while AK was away.

A woman entered the restaurant and sat at the table next to Ohm.

When AK returned Ohm asked, "I need another beer. Do you want one?" AK replied, "Yes, I've finished my beer. I feel lightheaded after bio break. I need another one."

"Okay, we'll order one." He ordered another beer.

After a few minutes, the waiter arrived with a wine and a beer. He placed the beer next to Ohm and gave Ohm the wine. Confused, Ohm said, "I didn't order wine. I ordered beer."

He heard a woman's voice from the table behind, saying, "I didn't order beer. I ordered wine."

Ohm turned to look at the woman's voice. A beautiful woman in her thirties was sitting at the table. She had fair skin and black hair.

Realizing the order mix-up, Ohm said, "No problem. Here's your wine." He took the wine glass from his hand and gave it to her.

She took the wine, handed him the beer, and said, "Thanks, here's your beer." Ohm smiled and took the beer.

She asked Ohm, "Indian?"

He replied, "Yes."

She said, "I'm from India too. If you don't mind, you can join me."

"With pleasure," Ohm said. He and AK sat at the table.

The lady said, "Just give me a minute to pay for the wine. I have a habit of paying in advance. Sometimes my card acts up."

Hearing this, AK was surprised and looked at Ohm, saying, "You're not Ohm Krishna; you're Shri Krishna. Just like you said, I've found someone who thinks like you."

The lady was confused and asked Ohm what was happening.

Ohm explained the conversation between two. The lady Smiled. Meantime waiter came to the lady with card machine and swiped her card and requested the waiter to play her favourite song. HE agreed and went.

The lady continued to Ohm.

"It happens sometimes. People think alike, and everyone has their own way of doing things. By the way, what's your name?"

"I'm Ohm Krishna, and he's Arun Kumar. We're both from Mumbai," Ohm said.

"Oh, nice. I'm from Indore, and my name is Prachi Guera," she replied.

Ohm got a little surprise. "Prachi Guera? You said you are from MP, and your name seems like a South American surname."

"Oh... that one... My father is a communist and he is an ardent follower of Che Guevara's principles. So in remembrance, he named me Prachi Guera."

"Good to hear. What are you doing in Germany? Basically, I am a software engineer. I work for one of the leading firms. You guys are here for a visit?"

"Yeah, we are here for a trip and the job got completed today. We need to plan for tomorrow."

"Oh, that's nice. There is a castle in Nuremberg. You can visit that."

While discussing, she got a call and was talking something serious in German before disconnecting the call

"Sorry guys, there's some electricity issue at my home. I need to go. "

"Take care, bye"

She left the hotel. After she left, AK told Ohm, "She lied to you. Her name isn't Prachi, and she's a south Indian"

Ohm was surprised and asked AK, "How do you know that?"

"I saw her credit card. It was written as Shiva Shankari, and it's a South Indian name." said AK

"What is the need for her to lie to us? She may have brought someone else's card." Ohm replied

"How is that possible?" asked AK.

"Did you see my card?" He showed his credit card to AK and said, "What is it written on it?"

OK read it and said, "It is written as Ojas Kulkarni."

"Am I Ojas Kulkarni?... No... He is my friend and I brought his card."

"OK."

"Yes, I and my friend both are OK. He is Ojas Kulkarni and I am Ohm Krishna, both are OK, right?"

"Sorry, yaar," AK felt a little guilt

. "Don't judge everything and go to conclusions without analysing anything."

AK was feeling bad and wanted to change Ohm's mood. He was looking at the TV, and the song "Hawa Hawa" from Rockstar was playing on it.

AK asked Ohm, "Ohm, look at this. What a beautiful place they shot this song! What a scenery! Is there any similar place we can visit here?"

"Proč hledáte podobné místo? půjdeme na stejné místo." Ohm replied in czechian language

AK did not understand anything and asked again please tell me clearly

Ohm replied "it means, why you are looking for a similar place? We will go the same place"

"What you mean?" AK surprised as usual

"Jedeme do Prahy" Ohm replied in the same language.

"What do you mean?" AK asked, confused.

"Tomorrow," Ohm said, creating suspense.

"Hmm, tomorrow?" AK couldn't contain his excitement.

"We will go to the same location, Prague."

"What?"

"Jedeme do Prahy - **Let's go to Prague.**"

CHAPTER ELEVEN

Unity In Diversity

It was 4:30 AM.

AK was sound asleep in his room, his snoring echoing like a diesel motor.

Ohm rang the room's calling bell. After thirty seconds of no response, he rang it twice more.

Another twenty seconds passed with no answer, so he rang it three times.

Ten seconds later, the bell began to ring continuously.

Finally, after a thirty-second onslaught of noise, AK was jolted awake and opened the door.

"Yes Ohm"

"Get ready. We need to leave in another 20 minutes"

"Where"

"Prague"

"At this time?"

"Yes. Otherwise, we won't be able to return on time. I've already booked the tickets. We need to start from Hauptbahnhof at 6:00 AM. Get ready."

Hauptbahnhof means central station.

It would take those 20 minutes to reach the Hauptbahnhof from their location.

AK took another 40 minutes to get ready.

They started at 5:20 AM and arrived at the Hauptbahnhof at 5:45 AM.

Ohm and AK were waiting at the bus station.

"Ohm, are we traveling by bus?"

"Yes," Ohm replied.

"How long is Prague from here?" AK asked.

"It's 300 kilometres, but it's in a different country. It's Czech Republic, next to Germany," Ohm explained.

"Okay," AK nodded.

The bus to Prague arrived. It was a Flixbus.

Both of them boarded the bus.

Unfortunately, they didn't get adjacent seats.

Ohm had booked the tickets last minute, so the available seats were scattered.

As a result, AK ended up in the third row while Ohm was seated in the seventh row.

Both of them secured aisle seats. AK's seat neighbour was an old man who snored really loudly.

It's funny because people who snore don't know how loud they are while they're sleeping.

They sleep peacefully even though their snoring is bothering other people.

AK was facing an uncomfortable situation and it was annoying, but AK tried to sleep anyway.

Whether you do something on purpose or by accident - **Karma is always like a boomerang.**

The bus stopped for a break. Ohm woke up AK, and they both got off the bus to buy food. They bought burgers and coffee for 600 Czech Kronas, Ohm tapped his card and paid the money.

Noticing the price, AK asked Ohm, "Have we reached the Czech Republic?"

"Since it's a tourist country, there are fewer security checks. Also, if you arrive by plane from outside of Europe, you have to go through immigration. But we're traveling within Europe, so there's no need for security checks here"

While having conversation in front of the bus AK notices the sign board in the bus

'Paris - Luxembourg - Nürnberg-Praha-Wroclaw-Krakow'

He asked, "Ohm, what is this? Is this bus coming from Paris?"

"Yes, this bus starts from France, passes through Luxembourg, enters Germany, then moves to Czech Republic, and finally reaches Poland. Wroclaw and Krakow are in Poland. This bus travels through five different countries," Ohm explained.

"How is that possible?" AK asked, amazed.

"Infrastructure in Europe is very good. They have a great public transportation system," Ohm replied.

"So you mean to say, if we have a good infrastructure, a person from Kolkata could go to Thailand via Bangladesh and Myanmar by bus?" AK mused.

"Yes, we need a good infrastructure as well as unity,"

CHAPTER TWELVE

VÍTEJTE V PRAZE

The bus was entering into Prague City.

A large board welcoming them in Czech, "Vítejte v Praze" (Welcome to Prague), greeted them.

The city's roads were a network of tram lines with trams constantly passing by.

The city's heritage was beautifully preserved. It was a stunningly clean and old city.

Bus travelled almost fifteen minutes inside the city and reached Florenc Bus station. Which is central bus station of Prague.

Both of them got down from the bus. Prague is much colder than Germany.

Ohm pulled out a printed tourist map from his bag.

Surprised, AK asked, "When did you buy this?"

"My seatmate was a travel vlogger from Istanbul. He was working in France and heading to Krakow for a job. We chatted, and he gave me this map with some recommendations," Ohm explained.

"That's impressive, but you're shameless! You talk to anyone without hesitation," AK joked.

"That's a basic qualification for a salesperson," Ohm replied, and they both laughed

Ohm headed towards the bus station exit and followed the map and signs to the nearest metro line. AK Followed him

Rabbit was following the Rhinoceros in the Unfamiliar Land.

Ohm reached the metro and approached the ticket machine and examined the options.

Finding no English language option, he used his Google Lens app to translate the content.

He purchased two tickets and he informed AK, "This is a day ticket, costing 5.5 Euros. We can use any mode of transportation in the city for the next 24 hours."

Surprised, AK asked, "Can we get a similar ticket to travel to Germany?"

"I already told you," Ohm replied.

"What?" AK feigned confusion.

"Change your mind-set," Ohm joked.

"Come on, Ohm, I'm just kidding," AK laughed.

They entered the metro and boarded the Line B train, alighting at the Můstek station.

As they exited, Ohm pointed to his right, "See that? That's the National Museum." It was a very big museum build with old heritage architecture and it looked like a palace I India

Both were impressed by the museum's beautiful architecture and took several pictures before continuing their exploration.

AK, unsure of their destination, asked Ohm, "Where are we going?"

"We're going to see the Astronomical Clock," Ohm replied.

"What's that?" AK inquired.

"The Prague Astronomical Clock is the third oldest heritage clock. Apart from the time, it displays the day, month, and positions of the sun, moon, and stars. It is the only heritage clock of its kind still operating in the world."

AK was really excited to see the clock.

After walking for another five minutes, they arrived to a plcae. Ohm raised hi hand and told AK , see that the astronomical clock.

OK was looking above and found there is clock in the top of the building Sun Moon and stars position in the dial. IT was around 10:55

They waited for five more minutes until the clock rang.

When the clock chimed, they watched it and took some pictures.

AK was overjoyed, exclaiming to Ohm, "This place is absolutely stunning! I'm so happy to be here. Thanks for this moment." A blend of Excitement and innocence was mixed in his feelings

Ohm has started accepting his innocence and he replied with a grin, "Don't get too excited yet, there are still two more places to see."

l

CHAPTER THIRTEEN

THE BRIDGE & THE CASTLE

The Bridge:

Ohm began walking away from the Astronomical Clock towards Charles Bridge.

They had already covered about three and a half kilometres that day.

AK's stomach started rumbling, and he asked for food.

Ohm reassured him, "Don't worry, I'll take you to an Indian restaurant. But first, enjoy this view." Ohm pointed to his right. It was Charles bridge.

The Charles Bridge is a remarkable structure, built between 1357 and 1402 under the reign of King Charles IV.

This 660-year-old bridge boasts 30 baroque sculptures and is renowned as one of the world's most beautiful and scenic bridges.

AK looked in the direction Ohm indicated and realized it was the same location from the Rockstar movie.

He didn't believe the words of AK when he told yesterday about let us go to the same place. Now he feels very happy and thank full to ohm

Overwhelmed with excitement, he immediately video called his friends.

The real-life view was even more breath taking than the movie.

He couldn't believe his eyes and took countless pictures.

Ohm was feeling happy inside by seeing the happiness of AK.

The best ever happiness in the world is to make someone happy.

They spent thirty minutes on the bridge before heading to an Indian restaurant. It was a small place with a few customers inside. Ohm approached an Indian old man overseeing the staff.

"Hello sir, we're from India. I've heard this is one of the best Indian restaurants in Prague. Do you serve all types of Indian food?" Ohm asked with a polite voice.

"Of course, sir. From South Indian dosa to Punjabi dal tadka, we have everything," the Old man replied.

""Great. We'll wait for the crowd to thin out. We'd like to order veg biryani. I'll pay in advance as my card sometimes gives me trouble," Ohm said.

Old man smiled on him and said "No problem sir. Please wait"

Fifteen minutes later, they enjoyed their veg biryani. While it wasn't the best Indian food Ohm had ever tasted, it satisfied their hunger. As they finished, the old man approached them and said

"I hope you enjoyed your meal, sir,"

"Yes, it was delicious. I'd like to buy something for my family. Do you have any suggestions?" Ohm asked.

"You should buy Prague wood sculptures. They're small but meaningful. There's a shop near the castle run by my friends. Here's my card. Show it to them for a discount," the old man offered his visiting card to him.

"Thank you so much," Ohm replied gratefully.

After finishing their meal, they left the restaurant.

"Ohm, what's next?" AK asked.

"We'll go to the castle. It's on a hill, so we'll have a great view of the city. Then we'll visit the shop to buy some toys and sculptures before we leave," Ohm explained.

The castle:

The castle was a little far from the bridge. They took tram number 22 and arrived at the castle in 20 minutes.

It took them another 15 minutes to reach the city viewpoint from the entrance.

The view from the top was really amazing.

The whole city looked orange because of the red roofs.

Ohm and AK were so amazed by the view that they forgot about everything else.

They sat down on a chair and talked about their old memories.

After this long journey, they both liked this place.

A connection formed between them, and a fragile bond of friendship began to develop.

It seems that understanding someone doesn't require years;

Sometimes, some bad situations and shared experiences are enough to build a strong relationship.

After their trip, Ohm and AK had become good friends.

They didn't mean to, but their time together made them close.

When they left the beautiful castle, they felt sad to go

Ohm started calling AK as Arun "Arun we will buy some toys from the shop"

"Sure Ohm"

Ohm and Arun went to the shop.

Ohm bought two toys and a sculpture.

He showed the restaurant owner's card and got a discount.

They said goodbye to the shop owner and took a tram to the bus station to catch the bus to Nuremberg.

The bus arrived on time, and they departed Prague.

As the bus moved forward, their minds travelled back to the unforgettable beauty of the city.

CHAPTER FOURTEEN

THE TERMINAL

Nuremberg:

Nuremberg: It was 4:30 AM. Arun and Ohm checked out of the room and caught a train to Nuremberg Airport.

They reached Nuremberg Airport on time. They took a bus from Nuremberg to Munich.

They reached Munich on time. Both of them had a burger and cappuccino at Starbucks. Ohm paid 58 euros with his card.

There were no problems during the departure process. Arun helped Ohm get the boarding passes. After getting the boarding passes Rabbit and Rhinoceros walked together.

After they got their passes, they went to the duty-free shop. Ohm bought a Davidoff Game On perfume on sale, and Arun bought Davidoff coffee for his home.

Ohm paid with his card, while Arun paid in cash.

The flight was announced, and they both boarded the plane.

Arun fell asleep and started snoring loudly, disturbing Ohm.

Arun slept and started his snoring over the nations. Ohm got disturbed because of him.

After six hours, Powai lake was looking into the sky and the plan was crossing the lake.

In another Few minutes , again it ran like ussain bolt in his finishing line and landed in the airport.

After few minutes both of them get down form the plane

.

Ohm and Arun went to collect the Chivas they had ordered before their departure.

An idea popped into Ohm's head, and he called Arun.

"You're allowed to buy two bottles from duty-free. I've already bought two. Since you're with me, can I buy two more using your boarding pass?" Ohm asked.

"Why are you asking, Ohm? Take this," Arun replied, handing over his boarding pass. Ohm bought another two bottles of Chivas and paid using his card.

Both of them collected the baggage and crossed the Exise inspection and came to the terminal exit area.

"Arun said, 'I'm going to take an Ola. Should I drop you off?'"

"No, Arun. I've informed my brother, and he's already at the airport," Ohm replied.

"Okay, bye then," Arun said. They both left the airport.

Powai lake was looking enjoying hte view of naked sky.

END OF THIS STORY.

A terminal is a place where the journey, ends but if you turn around, it becomes the start of a new one.

The Most important thing is how we are looking into the things.

Actually this Terminal does not ends this story. Let us turn the page.

***

3

**

2

*

1

The Parallel Story

This plot has a parallel narrative.

From Chapter 15

CHAPTER FIFTEEN

M-A-M

8th of this Month

PMO India

It was a Top level confidential meeting between The Prime Minister, The Home Minister and Defence general Vikram.

Defence General started "Sir we know the war situation between Russia and Europe. We are in friendship with both the Regions and we neither support or nor oppose both of them.

I have placed some secret codes of our army in several nations. Ukraine is one among them. Before the war initiated I have already moved this from Ukraine to its adjacent nations, but still it is in Europe.

We need to move those codes from Europe or bring back to the nation"

Home Minister said "Ok. Use our agents from Europe and get the codes"

Vikram Continued "There is a problem in it sir. Our Agents are under radar. It is very difficult to move them"

Home minister surprised and asked "How is that possible"

"Due to war universal radar is ON. Each and every countries Agents are under radar for the security purpose. If the codes went to any one of the region and then we need to support them. So it is very important to get back the codes without the knowledge of two regions" Vikram explained the situation clearly

"What is your plan?" Home minister asked

"I need to initiate the Sleeper Mission" Vikram replied

"You mean to say MaM?" home minister asked doubt fully

"Yes sir" Vikram said confidently

Turned towards the PM and Home minister asked "Sir what is your opinion"

"Vikram is Right. It is the right time to activate our invisible mission. Go ahead Vikram and bring back the codes and give me good news soon I want to monitor this mission personally, Start immediately"

"Jaihind Sir" Vikram stood and saluted the both.

Prime minister and home minister Stood and salute back and said "Jai hind"

Mission MaM is - **Man among Men**

CHAPTER SIXTEEN

A MAN THE AMONG MEN

MaM Control Room. It is filled with supercomputers, a non-traceable internet connection, and access to almost every corner of the nation and most parts of the world.

There are 25 technicians and 5 supervisors who are directly under the control of the Defence General. Including the PMO and Home Minister, this mission is run by 33 members.

Except for these 33 members, nobody knows where this control room is. It could be in the Himalayas, or it might be in the desert, or it could be in the sea; nobody knows

The purpose of the mission is to develop a parallel team to our secret spies to protect them, collect information, and transfer it. Even secret agents are unaware of this team.

Under the MaM mission, several agents are trained and deployed in the nation as sleeper cells.

There will be no direct communication with them. They live ordinary lives. The control room will activate them when needed. There will be no trace of their work.

Let's start the first mission:

The Defence General is in the control room now.

He called his team and said, "We need to start the mission now".

He called one of his best men, Raveender, and told him, "You have to lead this mission."

Raveender is one of the five supervisors of the team and the nation's best spy. He was assigned to the mission.

"What's the target sir?" Raveender asked Vikram

"Target is to get back a Parcel from Ukraine. I've already moved the Parcel to Poland. We need to send someone to collect the parcel from there." vikram replied

"Give me an hour sir. I'll come up with a plan." Raveender replied

After an hour, Raveender met Vikram and asked. "Sir, if I request to move the parcel from Poland, is it possible?"

Vikram replied "Yes. I can move to a neighbouring country within 24 hours, but beyond that, it's not feasible."

"That's more than enough, sir then we will start the project tomorrow"" said Raveender.

"Where should I move the parcel, and who are you sending?" vikram asked with a curiosity

"You should move the parcel to Prague in Czech, and I'm going to send 'The Good Salesman'"

Vikram smiled with a confident and said - "Good Choice"

CHAPTER SEVENTEEN

"The Good Sales Man"

MOM Control room:

9th of this Month;

Vikram was discussing with Raveender

"What is the plan, Ravi?" vikram Asked

"Sir, please move the parcel to Prague today. Our good Salesman is going to Germany in Airbhaarat today for his regular work, so we can use him to collect the parcel. As you know, this is a no-contact mission to evade enemy radar. There will be no communication with him, digital or analogue, throughout the operation," Raveender explained.

"Yeah, I know. Go ahead," Vikram replied.

"We've already informed Air Bhaarat to delay the flight without notifying passengers. Airlines usually inform passengers about delays, but we're making an exception. We're discreetly informing our salesman about a mission coinciding with his regular travel, and we're awaiting his acceptance."

"What's the tracking mechanism?"

"We'll use his credit card, sir."

After noticing the unexpected flight delay, Ohm Krishna realized an upcoming mission. He went to the duty-free shop and swiped his dedicated credit card.

A technician informed him, "The salesman has accepted the mission. He swiped his card at the duty-free shop."

"Okay, tell Airbhaarat to display the departure time"

He noticed the departure time was updated after the swipe, signifying mission initiation..

Upon arriving in Germany, Ohm Krishna swiped his card at Starbucks.

"Sir, the salesman has reached Germany and is awaiting his acceptance to launch" the technician reported.

Ohm Krishna swiped his card multiple times in Nuremberg.

"Sir, the salesman is in Nuremberg. He is on his regular work. Still awaiting his acceptance to launch," the technician reported.

Acceptance to launch is confirmed by swiping the card at an any Indian restaurant in the foreign nation.

Ohm Krishna is prepaying at the Indian restaurant using his card, signalling his readiness for the next step in the mission.

He swiped the card in Part E Restaurant

"Sir Salesman is ready to launch"

"Ok then send Shiva Shankari to the Restaurant"

Code to identify the same agent is swiping the card earlier. Both identify themselves.

Ohm captured the next city with the name of the spy Prachi Guera

PRAchi GUEra It is Prague.

To pinpoint the city and exact location, she demanded the hotel to play a Rockstar song as a clue to the destination.

He booked a ticket to Prague using his credit card.

"Sir Salesman will reach Prague tomorrow," said the technician.

"I will inform Vikram sir," Raveender replied.

Raveender informed Vikram about the salesman's arrival.

Ohm Krishna found three locations in the song. He explored these locations and discovered an Indian restaurant near Charles Bridge. He then used his credit card there.

"Sir Salesman is in Prague restaurant now" Raveender reported to Vikram

Vikram said, "No issues. The restaurant is owned by our mission's backend team. They will manage it from now on,'"

He obtained a card from the old man at the restaurant and went to a shop using the same card. There, they recommended a wooden sculpture. That is the parcel contains embedded secret codes with a non-traceable mechanism. He acquired the items and used his card for payment.

"Salesman collected the material" Technician reported to Raveender.

To ensure his return Ohm Krishna swiped his card in Starbucks at Munich Airport

"Salesman is started from Germany. Awaiting his confirmation on boarding"

To confirm the boarding salesman Swiped purchased perfume and swiped his card in Duty free shop at Munich Airport.

"Salesman is Confirmed his boarding. There is an Air Bhaarat Flight starting from Munich to Mumbai in 20 minutes"

To inform his arrival in India, Ohm Krishna purchased two more bottles of liquor at the duty-free shop with Arunkumar Boarding pass and used his card.

"Salesman is at Mumbai Airport," Technician reported Raveender said. "Send our vehicle to pick him up."

Ohm Krishna bid farewell to Arunkumar and headed to the parking lot.

There, he spotted a taxi with the number MH 14 AG 1947 - the date of India's independence, which was the code for delivering the material.

Ohm Krishna got into the car, handed the parcel to the driver, and said, "Jai Hind"

Mission ends successfully, but the story continues. Please turn the page.

CHAPTER EIGHTEEN

PART II

<u>The Introduction</u>

PMO - 15th of the same month

Prime Minister: "Good job, Vikram, and my special thanks to your team."

"Thank you, sir," replied the Vikram.

"I have a question," the Home Minister asked.

"Yes, sir," replied the General.

"You have moved the parcel from Poland to Prague. Then why haven't you moved it to Germany? It would be further easier, right?" Home minister asked with a curiosity.

"Sir, Prague is a tourist city with fewer immigration formalities. But Germany is a bit more difficult. So, to avoid risks, we kept the parcel in Czech Republic and sent our salesman to collect it. Even our salesman faced a tough situation in getting the visa approved in Germany. With his presence of mind, he managed to get it."

"I understand. What if his visa had been rejected in Germany? What was your Plan B?" the Home Minister asked.

Vikram smiled and said, "Salesman was not alone, sir."

"What?" Home Ministers curiosity increased further.

"Yes. We have another man as a backup called Arunkumar alias AK. He is another trained agent & he is the backup for Ohm Krishna. As Ohm Krishna swiped his card first, he did not swipe his card in the entire mission. If Ohm had not gotten the visa, Arunkumar would have swiped his card in Nuremberg.

His code name is 'The Bad Designer' "

The Bad Designer

"Don't worry about the finishing , it is very important how you are going to start. if you started with your whole heart, the universe will help you to finish it on its own way"
- Annamalai Shanmuganathan